At **THE DAVID BECKHAM ACADEMY** every day is a footballing adventure. Boys and girls come along to learn about the sport, develop their skills and have fun. But it's not just about tricks and flicks . . . As David Beckham knows, the real secret behind being a Premier League player is understanding the importance of dedication, teamwork, passion and having belief in yourself. In these pages you can meet football-mad children and follow them as they live out their dreams at The Academy.

SO STEP INSIDE AND JOIN THE FUN!

Want to know what some of our readers thought of this book?

'I think the best part is when Charlie meets Arthur and then catches the cup'

George, age 11

'Charlie was funny!'

Ryan, age 7

'My favourite character was Big Ben'

Hattie, age 9

'I liked Charlie's ability to save loads of goals'

Jordan, age 10

'My best thing was when Charlie catches the trophy and when he gets the phone call from David Beckham'
Jake, age 8

'I like Charlie because he is very confident'
Stephen, age 10

'I enjoyed the bit when Charlie saves Woody's free kick'
Joe, age 9

'I liked the character Big Ben – cool name!'
Jude, age 7

EGMONT

We bring stories to life

First published in Great Britain 2009
by Egmont UK Limited
239 Kensington High Street, London W8 6SA

Text and illustrations © 2009 Beckham Brand Ltd
adidas, Predator, the 3-Bars and the 3-Stripes are registered
trademarks of the adidas Group, used with permission

Text by Tommy Donbavand
Cover and inside illustrations by Adam Relf
Cover photography by Anthony Mandler
Design by Becky Chilcott

ISBN 978 1 4052 4526 5

5 7 9 10 8 6 4

A CIP catalogue record for this title is available
from the British Library

Typeset by Avon DataSet Ltd, Bidford on Avon, Warwickshire
Printed and bound in Great Britain by the CPI Group

THE DAVID BECKHAM
ACADEMY

SAVE THE DAY

EGMONT

CONTENTS

CONTENTS

SEARCH AND RESCUE

'This is ridiculous!' moaned Charlie as he tipped the laundry basket over his bed. 'Where *are* they?' He rummaged through dirty socks and T-shirts, chucking aside anything that didn't have blue stripes and five fingers – which was everything.

'My gloves have got to be here *somewhere!*' he continued as he tossed the basket to one side and dropped to the floor, wriggling on his stomach to explore the darkness beneath his bed. Unfortunately, all he found were a couple

of football stickers from last season's collector's album and the mouldy remains of an apple core.

Sliding out from under the bed, he tossed the apple core into the wastebasket then, after a second's thought, emptied the bin on to the floor and began to search through its contents.

'Have you seen my goalkeeping gloves

anywhere, Bob?' he asked the only other occupant of the room. 'I can't go to The David Beckham Academy without them!'

Bob sat in silence and watched as Charlie dragged the duvet and pillows off his bed, pushing a hand between the sheet and the mattress to feel around. But then Charlie hadn't really expected a reply in the first place – Bob *was* the family's pet cat.

'You're useless!' Charlie sighed as Bob curled up on the crumpled duvet and closed his eyes, but he crouched to scratch his pet behind the ears anyway. He scanned his bedroom as the cat purred softly.

The walls were covered with posters of football players and clippings of special matches cut from newspapers. In pride of place on the wardrobe door was a picture of his hero, David Beckham.

Charlie had been excited when his parents announced that they had booked him on a three-day course at The David Beckham Academy. He'd read in *Football Crazy* magazine that The Academy was putting together a special team, and he desperately wanted to wear the goalkeeper's shirt – and his lucky gloves, of course.

Charlie stared at the smiling face of David Beckham on the wardrobe. At the bottom of the poster was one of his hero's favourite sayings: 'Believe In Yourself'.

That's no help, Charlie thought. *How can I believe in myself if I can't find my – ah, the wardrobe!* He leaped to his feet suddenly. He hadn't looked on top of the wardrobe for his gloves. Dragging his bedside table across his room, Charlie pushed his alarm clock and copy of *Football Crazy* magazine on to the floor. There'd be plenty of time to tidy up when he returned as the official goalkeeper of The Academy's new team. Jumping on to the table, he stretched up to search the top of the wardrobe.

Charlie had always been small for his age, but that didn't matter when there were handy items of furniture around to give you a boost. He felt around the pile of board games and old toys – and that's when he heard the scream.

It wasn't the kind of scream you get when someone's watching a scary movie, or when your sister finds a spider in the bath. It was more like the scream you'd hear when your mum walked into your bedroom and discovered that you'd completely trashed it in less than twenty minutes flat. Still, it was enough to make Charlie lose his balance and fall. He toppled backwards, his arms windmilling wildly. Luckily, the thick duvet cushioned his fall – and Bob didn't even wake up.

'I didn't hear the explosion!' said Mum as Charlie scrambled to his feet and pulled the duvet back over his bed.

'What explosion?' asked Charlie.

'The bomb,' replied Mum. 'A bomb *has* gone off in here, hasn't it?'

'Sorry!' said Charlie. 'I just can't find my lucky gloves, and I'll never get into The Academy team without them.'

'It's just as well you made me pack them in your bag last night then, isn't it?' smiled Mum, straightening the duvet.

Charlie's cheeks flushed red as he remembered. 'I think I'm just nervous!'

'Not just nervous,' said Mum. 'You're late as well. Go and get in the car!'

As Mum followed Charlie down the stairs, Bob opened one eye and checked that he was finally alone. He yawned and settled back down to sleep. Peace at last!

● ● ●

On the way to The Academy, Charlie told his mum all about the special team the coaches were putting together. He told her how all the players would be picked from the kids training there over the coming weeks. By the time Charlie's mum dropped her son off at the entrance to The Academy, she was ready for a nap herself Charlie rushed inside, already pulling on his goalie gloves as he prepared for the best three days of his life.

Since he was a little late, he was handed his kit and asked to change quickly before being shown straight through to the pitch where the rest of his team was already gathered. He arrived just as the team's coach, Woody, was assigning positions to the group of eager young players in front of him. He paused as Charlie's tiny frame appeared beside him.

'You must be Charlie,' said the coach.

'We still need a defender and someone to play on the left wing. Which position would you prefer?'

'Neither – I'm in goal!' grinned Charlie as he waved his gloved hands in front of his face.

TIME TO SAVE

The rest of Charlie's team laughed.

'You?' barked a large boy from the back of the group. 'You're so small we're better off using you as a ball! And your gloves are ten sizes too big!'

'They were my dad's,' explained Charlie.

'And what did he use them for?' demanded the boy. 'Gardening?'

'Now, come on, Ben,' said Woody, resting a friendly hand on Charlie's shoulder. 'The gloves may be a little big on Charlie, but he's here because he loves football – just like everybody else. We teach players to respect each other at The David Beckham Academy.'

Charlie smiled. 'I want to earn their respect,' he said. 'I want to prove that I'm the best goalkeeper here.'

'And how are you going to do that?' asked Ben.

Charlie put his hands on his hips. 'By saving a free kick from each person here,' he said.

Woody thought for a second before replying. 'OK,' he said, 'I was going to warm you up with a little skills session but if Charlie wants to show us what he can do, we'll let him.' He glanced around the other groups of boys, huddling with their own coaches in various places on the pitch. 'We'll jog down to the away goal to take some free kicks while Arthur lays out some cones for our next drill.'

In the distance, the children could see an elderly man in overalls placing brightly coloured cones on the ground, whistling as he worked.

Charlie led the jog round the pitch towards the goal. As he ran, one of his teammates caught up with him.

'You don't have to do this,' he said.

Charlie looked up to find a tall, gangly boy on his left. 'Do what?'

'Prove anything to us, you know, just because you're small.'

'Don't worry, I'll be fine,' said Charlie, taking off one of his gloves to shake hands with the boy. 'My name's Charlie, by the way.'

'Liam,' came the reply. 'It's just that I know what it's like to, you know, look different to everyone else.'

'Me too,' grinned a stocky boy with flaming red hair on Charlie's other side. 'I *really* know what it's like to be teased with *my* hair!' The boy bowed dramatically. 'Thomas Walsh, at your service.'

Charlie laughed. 'Nice to meet you!'

'Ben was bragging to everyone that he's a natural keeper before you arrived,' said Liam. 'He even wanted us all to call him Big Ben. I think you put his nose out of joint.'

Thomas glanced over his shoulder at Ben's furious face. 'Nah,' he said, 'I reckon that nose has always been wonky!'

Reaching the goal, Charlie did a couple of quick stretches and pulled his gloves back on. Then he looked from post to post examining every centimetre of the ground in the goalmouth.

'Come on, Titch!' yelled Big Ben impatiently. 'Let's do it today!'

'That's enough!' ordered Woody. 'You OK, Charlie?'

'Fine,' replied Charlie. 'Just getting a feel for the space.'

The other boys laughed until Woody held up a hand to silence them. 'OK, Ben,' said the coach. 'When you're ready . . .'

Big Ben dropped the football a few metres outside the penalty area and took three steps back. Racing forwards, he struck the ball towards the top corner of the goal.

For a second, Charlie didn't move, then he leaped gracefully into the air and grabbed the ball in his hands, just before it could cross the line. Thomas and Liam started a round of applause as Ben's face turned a shade of purple.

'OK,' smiled Charlie, rolling the ball back out. 'Who's next?'

One by one, Charlie's teammates took free kicks from a range of positions and,

each time, Charlie stopped the ball with better and better saves. He jumped high, he lunged low, diving and blocking all types of shots with ease and never once fumbling the ball. Before long, all the boys had taken a shot and Charlie hadn't let in a single goal.

'Excellent work,' announced Woody. 'You've saved a free kick from everyone.'

'Not everyone,' said Big Ben. '*You* haven't taken a shot yet.'

'I really don't think it's appropriate for me to do that,' said Woody. 'We're not here to test out my skills and . . .'

'No, it's OK,' said Charlie. 'I'd like you to have a go.'

Woody reluctantly placed the ball down and stepped away from it, the team moving back to give him room. A silence fell across the pitch as the other teams, and even Arthur the caretaker, stopped to watch.

Glancing briefly up at the goal, Woody took his free kick. The ball whistled through the air, curling to the left as it zoomed towards the goalmouth. In the blink of an eye, Charlie dived to the side – arching his back and stretching his body as far as he possibly could – and pushed the ball wide with the very tips of his gloves.

The pitch erupted in noise as everyone cheered and clapped. From the centre, Arthur yelled, 'Go on, son!' and waved his arms triumphantly in the air. Ben turned away from the goal, sulking.

Thomas raced to Charlie's side. 'That was *amazing*!'

'It's like those gloves are magic!' said Liam.

Charlie felt his cheeks burn from the compliments. 'That's why I wear them every time I play,' he said. 'They're lucky.'

Woody grinned as he collected the ball from behind the net. 'I think we've found our goalkeeper!' he said.

SOMETHING'S MISSING

At the end of the first day's training, Woody announced that each of the groups at The Academy would be given a nationality to represent for the following day. Charlie and his team would be Brazil in the tournament against the other children.

'Cool!' beamed Charlie.

'That's it for today then,' said Woody with a sly smile, 'unless anyone fancies a quick tour of the Hall of Fame, that is . . .' The boys almost fell over each other as they raced excitedly for the door.

Soon they were crowding around a glass case displaying David Beckham's Manchester United shirt.

'Hey, look!' said Charlie excitedly as the rest of the team moved on further down the corridor. 'David Beckham's boots!'

Liam and Thomas joined him to stare in awe at the most famous footwear in football.

'Just think,' breathed Liam, steaming up the glass. 'Those boots scored some of the best goals in the history of football.'

Charlie nodded. 'I wouldn't fancy my chances of saving one of those shots!'

'That's why he won all these trophies,' said Thomas, pointing to the series of glass cabinets.

'I was hoping they'd have –' began Charlie, then he froze. 'That's not good.'

'What's not good?' asked Liam.

Charlie pointed to one of the cases. 'There's a trophy missing!'

● ● ●

The next morning, Charlie, Liam and Thomas whispered to each other as they put on their kits in the boys' changing room.

'I bet it was one of the other teams here that took the trophy,' said Thomas, pulling on his socks. 'I don't like the look of the kids playing for Spain.'

Liam shook his head. 'It's more likely to be, you know, someone with a grudge against David Beckham. Who's he scored the most goals against?'

'Whoever it was,' said Charlie as he laced his boots. 'It doesn't explain the smudges on the cabinet.'

'What do you think that was?' asked Thomas.

Charlie shrugged. 'It could be paint,' he suggested.

The boys fell silent as Woody strode into the dressing room. 'Come on,' he said. 'That's enough chatter! Let's get out there and practise some penalties.'

'Brilliant!' exclaimed Charlie, reaching into his bag. 'I love saving penalties!' His face fell. His goalkeeping gloves weren't there.

Charlie felt his eagerness begin to drain away.

⚽ ⚽ ⚽

Charlie stood on the goal line and trembled as Big Ben placed the ball on the penalty spot and took three steps back. He didn't feel right standing there without his lucky gloves on. He felt like his courage was missing.

He'd searched the dressing room for his gloves, hoping he'd put them down somewhere when he first arrived, and he'd even rung his mum to make sure he hadn't left them at home. There was no sign of them.

His friends stood behind the net, trying to encourage him. 'It's not the gloves that saved all those free kicks yesterday,' said Liam. 'It was you!'

'Yes, it *was* me,' agreed Charlie, eyeing the ball nervously. 'But I was wearing the gloves at the time!'

'They're just bits of material,' insisted Thomas. 'Pretty ragged bits too. They've got holes in the fingers.'

'It doesn't matter how ragged they are,' said Charlie. 'It's how *lucky*!'

'You'll be fine!' Liam reassured him as he backed out of the penalty area to let Ben take his shot.

Rushing up to the ball, he struck it with the inside of his boot, keeping the shot low towards the left of the goal. Charlie threw himself down . . . and fumbled. He felt the tough leather brush his fingers as the ball rolled into the back of the net.

'Yesss!' screeched Ben, punching his fist into the air. 'I got one past him!' He set off on a lap of honour round the pitch, shouting with joy.

'It's OK, Charlie,' said Woody as he replaced the ball on the penalty spot. 'I know the gloves mean a lot to you, but you can be

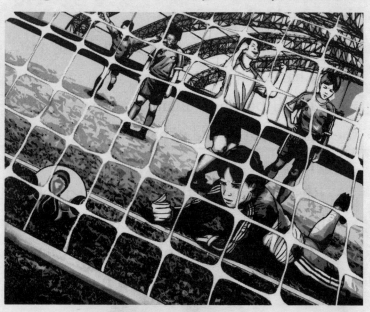

just as good a keeper without them.'

Charlie took a deep breath and tried to concentrate as the next player stepped up. This time the shot went straight between his legs. Penalty after penalty, Charlie failed to save a single ball as he tripped and staggered along the goal line. As his confidence disappeared he became more and more clumsy, until he began to look like a total beginner.

'I did it! I did it!' sang Big Ben as he ran past on the start of his third lap. The rest of the team didn't share his enjoyment, however. They glanced nervously at each other, wondering whether the magic they'd seen in Charlie's goalkeeping performance yesterday had truly vanished. Could the gloves really have been behind the incredible skill he had displayed?

'I-I'm just going to get some water . . .' said Charlie softly, trudging towards the changing rooms.

Woody nodded. 'Thomas, you're in goal for the minute.'

In the dressing room, Charlie slumped on to the bench and listened to the noise of the practice session out on the pitch. His dream was ruined. He'd never be picked for The Academy team now. Forcing back tears, he sagged forwards, resting his head in his hands.

That's when he noticed another black smudge.

THE GLOVES ARE OFF

'I'm telling you,' hissed Charlie as the Brazil team lined up alongside Sweden for the first game of the tournament. 'Whoever took that trophy also stole my gloves!'

Thomas grabbed his foot and pulled it up behind his back to stretch his leg muscles. 'No offence,' he said, 'but your tatty old gloves aren't exactly in the same league as one of David Beckham's trophies!'

'How are you feeling?' asked Liam.

'Like someone's sitting on my chest,'

replied Charlie. 'I can't believe how nervous I am!'

'Try not to think about it,' advised Liam as the referee led the teams out on to the pitch. 'Just concentrate on the game and you'll be fine.'

'I'd be better if I knew who'd taken my gloves,' snapped Charlie as he eyed members of the Sweden team to see if any of them looked guilty.

Taking up his place in the goal, Charlie swallowed hard as Sweden won the toss and kicked off. They attacked from the first moment, sending the ball wide to the left midfielder, who charged down the line before crossing the ball expertly into the penalty area. The Sweden striker leaped into the air and headed the ball at goal, aiming it low to Charlie's left.

Charlie flailed desperately as the ball rocketed between his hands and hit the back of the net. Sweden had scored within the first few seconds of the game, and he'd been responsible. He tried not to catch anyone's eye as the referee blew his whistle and the teams jogged back into their positions for the restart.

The rest of the match continued in much the same way. Every time Sweden attacked, Charlie either froze or fumbled for the ball as though he had never played a game in his entire life.

At one point, Sweden was awarded a corner and both teams crammed into the Brazil penalty area.

'I *must* get this!' Charlie growled to himself as the Sweden striker took the corner. The ball sailed over the heads of the players in the box as Charlie came rushing off his line, completely missing the ball and tripping over his own players. Grabbing his chance, one of the opposing team's midfielders chested the ball with ease and then thumped it into the empty net. Two–nil.

Charlie's teammates grumbled as they made their way back down the pitch. Even Thomas and Liam seemed to be annoyed at their friend's poor performance.

The game became more and more desperate as the Brazil players struggled to keep Sweden from getting anywhere near their goal. They knew Charlie had no chance of saving anything that got past the defensive line.

Thomas slid to rescue the ball from the Sweden striker, arriving a split second too late and earning Sweden a free kick from

midway inside Brazil's half. It was exactly the sort of attack Charlie had stopped again and again on the first morning of training. One of the opposing team's defenders stepped up to take the shot and curved the ball around Brazil's wall, straight towards the goalkeeper's hands. Charlie froze, and the ball bounced off his shoulder – and over the line.

'Oh, come *on*!' shouted Thomas angrily.

The final score was 5–1 to Sweden, and even Big Ben's goal in the dying minutes of the game did little, if anything, to raise the spirits of the losing team.

Charlie decided to skip the showers; he'd collect his stuff and get changed after everyone else had gone home. He just couldn't face the angry stares that were sure to await him in the changing room.

Instead, he set off for the Hall of Fame to try and find inspiration from some of his heroes.

'I just don't get it,' he said to David Beckham's Manchester United shirt as it hung silently in its glass display case. 'I *know* they're just gloves, and not even good gloves at that, but I *need* them to play well!' He paused, as if hoping that the Number 7 shirt would offer up some words of wisdom, but the Hall of Fame stayed silent.

'Listen to me,' he moaned. 'It was bad enough when I was talking to the cat at home – now I'm asking a football shirt for help!' He laughed at the stupidity of the situation. 'If I'm going to question a bit of kit, I should ask one of the boots – at least they've got a tongue!'

Charlie turned to the case containing

David Beckham's football boots and felt a cold shiver run down his spine. The case was empty, a dirty black fingerprint clearly outlined on the outside.

The thief had taken the boots as well! Surely the police would have to get involved now.

A noise at the end of the corridor made him jump. A man in overalls stepped out of the toilets shaking his hands dry after washing them. Charlie leaned back against the wall, trying not to be seen. He couldn't make out the man's face because he had his back to Charlie and was in shadow where one of the spotlights had blown.

He's broken the light to protect his identity, Charlie thought. *I have to tell somebody — and quickly.*

CALL FOR BACKUP

Charlie turned and raced back along the corridor. He knew that this man had stolen the trophy, David Beckham's boots *and* his lucky goalkeeping gloves. All he had to do was tell someone.

Turning the corner, he spotted the head coach's office and ran for the door. In the distance, he could hear the last of the children leaving for the night, chattering away about all the skills that they had learned that day. Charlie was nearly at the door when Liam and Thomas stepped suddenly out of the changing room. The boys crashed to the ground in a tangle of limbs.

'We were just coming to look for you,' said Thomas as he pulled his leg out from beneath Charlie's back. 'We thought you might be annoyed with us.'

'Yeah,' agreed Liam, flat on his stomach, 'but we didn't think you'd, you know, attack us as soon as we appeared.'

'I didn't attack you,' exclaimed Charlie as he climbed to his feet. 'I was going to see the head coach. I know who the thief is!'

'Are you still on about your missing gloves?' moaned Thomas.

'Not just my gloves,' said Charlie. 'The thief took the trophy and Beckham's boots as well! The police have to be called.'

'The problem with calling them,' said Liam, 'is that they need evidence.'

'I've *got* evidence!' grinned Charlie. 'A fingerprint! And I know who the thief is anyway,' he said as it all clicked into place in his head. 'Who's the only person we've seen wearing overalls at The Academy?'

Thomas and Liam replied at the same moment. 'Arthur!'

Charlie nodded excitedly. 'He's got access to the whole Academy.'

'Which means *he* must have left those smudges on the glass cabinets!' added Liam.

'This is big,' said Thomas. 'We need to tell the head coach!'

'That's what I was going to do when you two lurched out in front of me,' explained Charlie. He started for the coach's office door, but Liam grabbed his arm and stopped him.

'We just wanted to say, you know, sorry,' he said. 'We know it was hard for you to play without your gloves, and we shouldn't have got annoyed when you let so many goals in.'

Charlie smiled. 'That's OK,' he said. 'But now I have the chance to save something more important. Let's go!'

● ● ●

Frank Evans was putting the finishing touches to his plans for the new Academy team strip when the telephone rang.

As the head coach at The David Beckham Academy, he could have chosen the plushest office in the building, but he preferred to keep things simple. There were no expensive paintings or gadgets here: just functional furniture, a laptop computer and, of course, pictures of The Academy's founder.

'I'm glad you called,' Frank said, clicking the phone in front of him on to loudspeaker and settling back into his office chair. 'I've just seen the new strip design and I think you'll –' He was interrupted as the door crashed open and Charlie, Thomas and Liam burst in.

'We know who the thief is!' Charlie shouted.

Unfortunately, he was a little difficult to understand as all the boys were talking at once.

Frank raised a hand to silence them. 'Can't this wait?' he demanded sternly. 'I'm in the middle of a very important phone call!'

'Unless you're on the line to the police, no!' said Thomas. 'We know who stole the trophy.'

'And the boots!' added Liam.

'And my gloves!' said Charlie.

Frank studied the trio standing impatiently on the other side of his desk. 'I think you're making a mistake, boys,' he said more quietly. 'And this is a very important phone call. I'm talking to

David Beckham himself.' Liam's eyes widened at the mention of his hero's name and Thomas looked as though he might faint.

Only Charlie remained determined to get to the bottom of the mystery. He leaned towards the phone. 'Don't worry, we'll get everything back for you!' he announced. 'By the way, love the free kick you scored last weekend!' Then he ran out of the room, closely followed by his friends.

Frank Evans sat, stunned, for a second then continued his conversation.

● ● ●

'He didn't believe us!' exclaimed Charlie as he, Thomas and Liam dashed along the corridor towards the Hall of Fame. 'He thinks we're just crazy kids.'

'You *are* a crazy kid!' snapped Liam. 'You just interrupted a phone call with David Beckham!'

'Who will probably thank each of us personally for returning his stuff,' said Charlie as he pushed open the last door to the Hall of Fame. 'Mr Evans will *have* to believe us when we get the trophy back and show it to him.'

At the far end of the corridor stood Arthur in his overalls at the top of a ladder, with an assistant at the bottom holding it steady.

'There they are,' said Thomas.

'He's fixing the light and trying to cover up the evidence,' Charlie snarled.

'And look!' said Liam. 'He's got the missing trophy in his overall pocket!'

Charlie took a deep breath, then he

began to run along the corridor towards Arthur. 'Let's get him.'

CATCH OF THE DAY

Before Charlie could run more than two steps, Woody appeared from a side door, looking startled to see Academy students still there after hours.

'What are you boys doing?' he asked. 'Aren't your parents here yet?'

'It's him,' Charlie yelled, pointing at the caretaker on his ladder. 'He's stolen David Beckham's trophy and boots!'

'And your gloves,' reminded Thomas.

'And my gloves!' Charlie agreed.

At the far end of the Hall of Fame,

Arthur and Jason, his assistant, had just finished fitting the new light bulb when they heard a commotion.

'Here, Arthur . . . Isn't that the little lad that you said was the best young talent you'd seen since Peter Schmeichel?' asked Jason.

Arthur peered down the corridor past the shirts and football memorabilia that lined the walls. 'I think so,' he said. 'What's he still doing here?'

'I don't know,' said Jason, 'but he seems all worked up about something. He's shouting.'

'What's he saying?' asked Arthur.

'No idea,' said Jason. 'This place echoes like nobody's business.'

Back at the far end of the Hall of Fame, Charlie was refusing to be ignored by

Woody. 'He needs to give himself up and be put on trial!'

'What does that mean?' asked Thomas.

'I don't know,' Charlie admitted. 'I just heard it on one of the crime dramas my mum watches.'

'What *is* going on here?' demanded a voice. Charlie and Thomas turned to see Frank Evans striding towards them. 'Would you mind telling me what is so important that it's worthy of interrupting a telephone call to David Beckham?'

'Over there, Mr Evans,' said Charlie, pointing to Arthur. 'We've found the trophy!'

Thomas nodded.

'But that still doesn't explain why you seem to be accusing Arthur of stealing one of The Academy's trophies,'

Frank replied. 'He's a valued member of our maintenance team.'

'But he's got the trophy!' exclaimed Thomas.

'That's because I gave it to him,' said Frank. 'Or, at least, I gave him the keys to the display cabinet . . .'

Charlie's heart thumped as Frank Evans continued to talk. This was bigger than he thought; the maintenance team and the head coach were in it *together*! Perhaps they'd helped set up The Academy in a plot to steal valuable football memorabilia? What had gone missing before Charlie had even arrived?

'. . . and he very kindly agrees to take the trophies home once a month to polish them.'

The words slammed Charlie back

to reality. 'I'm sorry,' he whispered. 'Could you please repeat that last bit?

Frank sighed. 'Arthur takes the cup home once a month to polish it!'

Charlie felt his cheeks begin to burn again. 'So he's not trying to steal it?'

'Of *course* not!' scoffed the head coach. 'We check our employees very carefully before they're allowed to work here.

Everyone, especially Arthur, is completely honest.'

'The boots!' blurted Liam. 'Someone's taken them as well!'

Frank Evans smiled. 'The trophies aren't the only things that need polishing,' he said. 'Arthur's got those too. He uses the finest boot polish to keep them gleaming in their cases!' At the words 'boot polish', the three boys gulped. They had obviously made a terrible mistake.

'Come on,' said Woody. 'I'll introduce you to him so that we can straighten all this out.'

The group trooped over to where the two maintenance staff were working and Woody cleared his throat to speak.

'Hi, Arthur. How's the cleaning coming along?'

'Fine thanks, Woody,' the old man replied. 'If it wasn't for this light bulb blowing I'd have done those cabinets by now. I've gone and got fingerprints all over them.'

'Well, these boys here wanted me to introduce themselves and ask you about that trophy in your pocket,' Woody said, a smile beginning to creep over his face.

'This one?' Arthur asked, reaching into his overall and producing the shiny cup.

'Yes. They seem to think that you wanted to steal it.'

Jason suddenly roared with laughter, letting go of the ladder in the process. It began to wobble and Arthur reached out to stop himself falling, dropping the trophy in the process.

Everyone watched as the cup fell, almost

in slow motion, from the top of the ladder.

'No!' yelled Arthur as he watched the trophy spin and fall.

Without hesitation, Charlie sprinted across the short distance to the ladder and dived at full stretch, grabbing the cup just before it hit the ground. He slid across the wooden floor of the Hall of Fame and carefully picked himself up, the cup now

firmly pressed to his chest. There was a second's stunned silence, then everyone roared with delight.

As Frank, Thomas and Liam joined Charlie to pat him on his back, Arthur climbed down from the top of the ladder to shake his hand. 'That was a pretty good save!' he grinned.

'Especially for someone who hasn't got his lucky gloves,' added Woody. 'I said you still had it in you!'

Charlie shrugged. 'I'm not sure . . .'

'Take it from someone who knows!' said Woody. 'As David Beckham always says: Believe In Yourself!'

ON THE SPOT

'There he is!' shouted a voice.

'Three cheers for Charlie!' yelled another. 'Hip hip!'

'Hooray!' roared everyone on the pitch.

'Hip hip!'

'Hooray!'

'Hip hip!'

'Hooray!'

Charlie blushed again as he walked out on to the pitch with the rest of the Brazil team. Ever since catching the trophy the day before, he'd become something of a celebrity around The Academy. A girl playing for the Argentina team had even asked for his autograph at lunchtime.

Now, however, he had more important matters on his mind. Brazil was about to play its final game in the tournament. Despite Charlie's poor performance in the opening match, he'd been back on form for that morning's matches. If the team beat Holland in this final game, Brazil would win the tournament. Holland just needed a draw.

'Do you think we can do it?' he asked Liam as they took their positions ready for the kick-off.

'If you can catch a trophy at full stretch, a football should be no problem at all!' came the reply.

As Charlie turned to make his way to the goal, someone tapped him on the shoulder.

It was Big Ben. 'Look . . .' he said, scraping the studs of his boots nervously on the turf. 'I was a bit of an idiot when I first got here, but . . .' The large boy swallowed hard. 'You're all right!'

As Ben dashed away to toss the coin, Thomas grinned in Charlie's direction. 'Looks like everyone's on your side now!'

Charlie glanced up at the banner of

David Beckham on the wall. His hero's advice was right. He just had to believe in himself.

Brazil won the toss and kicked off, making an early break down the right wing and knocking a high cross into the Holland penalty area. The Holland goalkeeper was, however, nearly as good as Charlie and he leaped above the sea of heads to claim the ball and stop the attack.

He kicked the ball out quickly, deep into the Brazil half. The Holland forwards raced towards it as Liam shouted instructions to Brazil's defence. Holland's striker dummied a shot, putting Liam off guard and giving him space to round the defender. The crowd cheered as he hammered a shot at goal.

Charlie had to jump high and to his right to make the save. It still felt strange, stopping shots without gloves, but he cleared his head of those thoughts as he tossed the ball back out.

It landed squarely at Thomas's feet and, with a quick burst of speed, he dribbled it past first one, then another player in the Holland team. Passing wide to the winger, he spotted a free route through the defence and arrived at the goalmouth just as the

cross came in to meet him. With a scorching header, Thomas took Brazil into the lead.

'Yesss!' Charlie punched the air happily as Thomas's teammates crowded round to congratulate their friend. So long as they could keep this lead, the trophy was theirs.

The game continued to be evenly matched with both Charlie and his Holland counterpart having to work hard to keep any further goals from being scored. Holland had been working on their set-piece free kicks during training and, as one of the shots curved round the wall and headed straight for the inside post of the Brazil goal, Charlie was forced into an incredible save, knocking the ball wide by a whisker.

With just minutes left on the clock, both teams crowded into the Brazil penalty area as one of the Holland midfielders prepared to take the corner. Charlie was easily the shortest player on the field, and he struggled to see anything through the forest of bodies crowded around him.

Everybody, defenders and attackers alike, jumped into the air as the ball approached. Charlie, aware that he didn't have the height to get above them and snatch the ball, stayed on his line, waiting to stop anything that came his way.

The ball came into view – and it was heading straight towards a tall Holland striker. This wouldn't be an easy save to make and, even if the shot came within Charlie's reach, he knew that there would be a lot of power behind it. He braced himself . . . but the striker was pushed to the ground.

The referee blew his whistle, calling the trainer on to the pitch to see to the injured player. Charlie scanned the box to find out who had committed the foul and was amazed to see Thomas looking embarrassed.

'You did that?' Charlie asked.

Thomas nodded. 'I didn't mean to,' he said. 'I just had my eye on the ball and didn't see him coming.'

With seconds of the match remaining, Holland had a penalty.

MAKING THE GRADE

Charlie was relieved to see that the Holland striker wasn't badly injured. He'd taken a bump to the bridge of his nose that had stunned him slightly, but his determination quickly returned as he stepped up to place the ball on the penalty spot.

The rest of the Brazil team members crowded around the penalty area, some of them not daring to watch. Charlie hadn't saved a single penalty since he had arrived at The Academy. Their dream of winning the tournament was squarely in their goalkeeper's hands.

Happy that the ball was in the best position possible, the Holland striker began to take several strides back as everyone held their breath.

'Stop!' shouted a voice. Woody was racing along the touchline towards Brazil's goal.

'What's going on?' demanded the referee.

'Can I have a quick word with Charlie?' Woody asked.

'Go on,' said the ref, 'but make sure it *is* quick.'

Woody dashed on to the pitch and pulled something from the pocket of his shorts. 'Look what I found,' he grinned.

'My lucky gloves!' exclaimed Charlie. 'Where were they?'

'They'd slipped down the back of the benches in the changing room,' explained Woody. 'Arthur found them when he was replacing one of the bolts that holds the benches to the floor.'

Charlie stared down at the gloves silently, running his fingers over the fading blue stripes that ran the length of the fingers.

'What's the matter?' asked Woody.

'I don't know what to do,' admitted Charlie. 'If I'd got these back yesterday, I'd have been jumping up and down with joy. But now I've been playing well without them . . .' He looked up at Woody. 'Should I wear them or not?'

'I can't decide that for you,' replied Woody. The referee blew his whistle to ask him to clear the pitch. 'It's up to you, Charlie.'

As Woody left the goalmouth, Charlie gripped the gloves tightly in his hands. He looked up at the impatient Holland striker, then thought of David Beckham's words: 'Believe In Yourself'. Charlie smiled and threw the gloves over the touchline. It was time to follow that advice!

The referee blew his whistle again and the Holland striker stepped up to take the penalty. The ball arced high and to the left; Charlie left the goal line a split second later. He watched the spinning football shoot directly for the gap between himself and the top corner of the net. Everything seemed to move in slow motion, just like it had when he'd had to dive to catch the falling trophy. But now he didn't just want to save the cup – he wanted to *win* it.

Crashing to the ground, Charlie slid to a stop, his arms clasped to his chest. For a second he didn't move, but slowly he sat up to reveal something nestled safely in his arms. It was the ball; he'd saved the penalty!

The referee blew his whistle to

signal the end of the game and the tournament. Brazil had won! Racing over to Charlie, his teammates surrounded him, cheering and shouting. Even the Holland players were applauding what had been a brilliant save.

Suddenly, there was Frank Evans, carrying the trophy in his direction. Smiling, the head coach began handing the cup to him — when someone grabbed Charlie's arm and dragged him out of the crowd. It was Woody.

'Phone call,' he said, passing a mobile over. Charlie sighed. He'd told his mum what time the game would end and when she had to pick him up! Watching enviously as Big Ben took the trophy and began another lap of honour round the pitch — this time joined by the rest of the team – Charlie pressed the phone to his ear.

'You're not going to shout at me again, are you?' said a familiar voice.

Charlie's eyes widened in surprise. It was David Beckham! 'Er . . . n-no! Sorry about that!'

'That's OK,' said David. 'You were trying to help The Academy at the time. Well, I wanted to speak to you to tell you that it needs your help again. We need you to play in goal for the new Academy team.'

Charlie couldn't believe what he was hearing. '*Really?*' he gasped.

'Woody tells me you'd be the perfect choice,' said David, 'and we'll even get you some new goalkeeping gloves . . .'

Charlie reached down to pick up the

gloves he'd put aside earlier. 'I'm not sure I need them anymore.'

'That's up to you,' said David. 'We've all got our superstitions to keep us playing well. In fact, Woody used to have a pair of tatty old boots he would never take off!'

Charlie grinned. 'I'll be sure to ask him about those!' He thanked his hero for the chance to play for the team and, most of all, for the advice that had helped him win the tournament, then he handed the phone back to Woody.

With a final glance down at the gloves, he stuffed them into the pocket of his shorts and raced off down the pitch to join the celebrations with the rest of his team. Maybe he'd keep the gloves in their own glass case in the corridor at

home from now on. He just had to think of a way to get Arthur to clean them once a month . . .

TURN THE PAGE TO READ A SNEAK PREVIEW OF

 BOSSY BOOTS

THE FOURTH BOOK IN
THE DAVID BECKHAM ACADEMY
SERIES!

SHOPPING SPREE

Tom dragged his feet across the driveway at a snail's pace. His mum and gran were already sitting in the car.

'Hurry up, Tom!' called his mum out of the window. 'We've got a *lot* of shopping to do!'

'Great,' groaned Tom. 'Lots of shopping. Remind me why I have to come again?'

Tom's gran giggled. 'We need a handsome young man to tell us which clothes suit us!'

'But I'm meant to be playing football

in the park,' he complained, climbing into the back seat. 'It's not fair!'

Tom lived with three girls – his mum, his big sister and his grandma. And the worst thing about it was being dragged on long, boring shopping trips all the time.

'You've played football every waking moment for the last nine days!' said his mum as they pulled away. 'A day off won't hurt you.'

'I bet David Beckham never had to put up with this kind of thing!' he moaned. 'How do you expect me to play for England one day when I have to spend my Saturdays looking at shoes or hats or . . . whatever you're going shopping for today?'

'Well, you'll just have to ask him when you're a famous footballer yourself,' laughed Tom's mum. 'Now, first stop is going to be the jewellery shops. I want to find a nice pair of earrings to . . .'

Tom tuned out his mum's voice and stared out of the window. It was physically impossible to listen to a conversation this boring. He imagined his mates must be picking teams right now. Whichever one he was on, he knew he'd be the star striker!

'Then, after four or five hours,' his gran was saying, 'we can move on to handbag shops . . .'

Tom let out another sigh. He was even wearing his football kit, complete with boots, ready to go and play. And now he had an entire day of standing outside changing rooms to look forward to.

'And then of course some shoe shops!' said his mum. Tom couldn't believe she actually looked excited at the thought of going to a shoe shop.

Their car pulled up at some traffic lights, and Tom looked out at the huge advertising billboard by the side of the road. It showed a famous footballer doing a dramatic overhead kick in a pair of dazzling football boots.

'Wow!' sighed Tom, gazing longingly at the poster. The boots were silver with special 'blade' studs. They looked a bit like something from outer space.

'And then in the second shoe shop, I want to . . .' droned Tom's mum.

Tom looked down at the mucky, frayed bits of leather on his feet. The stitching was coming away on the toes and the right boot had sticky tape wrapped round a hole in the heel.

'Mum, will any of the shoe shops sell football boots?' he interrupted.

His mum turned round with a frown. 'I'm not made of money, love.'

Tom's eyes widened. She could have fooled him with all this talk of jewellery and bags and shoes. It seemed she had read his mind.

'Sorry, darling. But the way you're growing they wouldn't last five minutes. Your gran and I are as big as we'll ever be. I hope!' she said, laughing at her own joke.

Tom rolled his eyes. There was *no way* he could put up with 8 hours of this. He pressed his nose against the car window – he liked this bit of the journey to town: they were driving past the back of The David Beckham Academy.

'Mum, one day, can I . . .' he began, but he didn't even finish his sentence. It wasn't even worth asking for a trip to The Academy, he decided. Not until nearer his birthday, and that was 10 months away!

'And then we can stop for a cup of tea, before looking at hats,' his gran was saying. He imagined the big pitches inside The Academy's arches, full of teams learning new skills and playing in great tournaments. And here he was, spending a day looking at hats. His mum turned the car off the main road and into a huge car park.

'*Muuum!*' Tom groaned. 'You've done it again. This isn't the way to town!'

Tom's mum smiled into the car mirror. 'Oh, this is the way all right!' she said. They were driving through a maze of parking spaces and fences.

'Er . . . it really isn't, mum,' said Tom. 'This is just like the time you nearly drove us to Wales by accident when we were going to the supermarket!'

'That was an easy mistake to make!' frowned his mum. 'It's just around this corner anyway.'

Tom's gran turned round in her seat and gave her grandson a wink. 'You know, your mum and I are hitting the shops today,' she said with a smile.

'Yes,' grumbled Tom under his breath.

'But you aren't coming with us!' she cried. 'We're dropping you off just over here!'

'But . . .' Tom said, puzzled. 'What am I going to . . . WOW!'

The car rounded a final corner and came to a stop — *right in front of*

The David Beckham Academy!

'You don't mean . . . am I going . . .?' Tom couldn't get his words out fast enough.

'Yes!' cried Tom's mum. 'You're going to spend three whole days in there, playing football until it comes out of your ears!'

'My treat!' said his gran. 'It's an early birthday present!'

Tom gasped and fumbled with the car door handle. 'You mean I'm going to . . .' The door burst open and he tumbled out head first, landing in a heap on the concrete. He looked up at the big glass doorway and turned back to the car with his mouth gaping.

'This is the best present *ever*!' he gasped. His gran leaned out of the car window and gave him a gentle push.

'Well, go on then,' she said. 'They'll be starting in a minute.'

Tom turned round and bounded towards the door. This was going to be *way* better than looking at hats!

Collect all the books in
The David Beckham Academy range

STORY BOOKS

1. Twin Trouble   ISBN 978 1 4052 4524 1   £4.99

2. Le Football   ISBN 978 1 4052 4525 8   £4.99

3. Save the Day   ISBN 978 1 4052 4526 5   £4.99

4. Bossy Boots   ISBN 978 1 4052 4527 2   £4.99

and coming soon in spring 2010 . . .

5. Away From Home   ISBN 978 1 4052 5164 8   £4.99

6. Captain Incredible   ISBN 978 1 4052 5165 5   £4.99

ACTIVITY BOOKS

How-to Handbook   ISBN 978 1 4052 4669 9   £4.99

Ultimate Football   ISBN 978 1 4052 4670 5   £4.99
Sticker Book

ANNUAL

2010 Annual   ISBN 978 1 4052 4644 6   £7.99